Donald Crews
Parade

Greenwillow Books/New York

For all of you
I always remember
and for any of you
I sometimes forget

Library of Congress Cataloging in Publication Data

Crews, Donald. Parade.

Summary: Illustrations and brief text present the various elements of a parade—the spectators, street vendors, marchers, bands, floats, and the cleanup afterwards.
1. Parades—Juvenile literature.
[1. Parades—Pictorial works]   I. Title.
GT3980.C73   1983   394'.5   82-20927
ISBN 0-688-01995-1
ISBN 0-688-01996-X (lib. bdg.)

NO PARADE TODAY PARKING

**Buttons,
balloons,
and flags
for sale.**

**Hot dogs,
pretzels,
ice cream,
and soda
to buy.**

ICE CREAM

CANDY

SODA

Watchers gather.

A crowd.   Waiting.

Here it comes!

Flags
flying.

A strutting
drum major
leads the
marching band.

Trombones, clarinets, saxophones,

cornets,

trumpets, flutes,

French horns.   **sousaphones,**

field drums, cymbals, and last the big bass drums.

and baton twirlers, twirling and turning.

Bicycles from bygone days,

and antique
automobiles,

a cruise ship,

and at the end
of the parade,
the brand-new
fire engine.

**Nothing left
to see,
nothing left
to do except . . .**

clean up.